THE
EASY CLASSICS
EPIC COLLECTION

Published by Sweet Cherry Publishing Limited
Unit 36, Vulcan House,
Vulcan Road,
Leicester, LE5 3EF
United Kingdom

First published in the UK in 2021
2021 edition

2 4 6 8 10 9 7 5 3 1

ISBN: 978-1-78226-787-4

The Easy Classics Epic Collection: Fathers and Sons

Based on the original story by Ivan Turgenev,
adapted by Gemma Barder.

Cover design by Helen Panayi and Dominika Plocka
Illustrations by Helen Panayi

Lexile® code numerical measure L = Lexile® 720L

www.sweetcherrypublishing.com

Printed and bound in Turkey
T.IO006

FATHERS AND SONS

Ivan Turgenev

Sweet Cherry

THE KIRSANOVS

Nickolai Kirsanov
Head of the family

Arkady Kirsanov
Son

Fenichka
Nickolai's fiancée

Kolyazin
Arkady's cousin

THE BAZAROVS

Doctor Bazarov
Head of the family

Mrs Bazarov
Wife

Yevgeny Bazarov
Son

THE ODINTSOVS

Anna Odintsov
Wealthy widower

Katya Odintsov
Anna's sister

Fifi
Katya's dog

CHAPTER ONE

Nickolai Kirsanov was waiting impatiently at the train station. He stared down the tracks, willing the train to come. His son, Arkady, would be on the train, coming home after graduating from St Petersburg University. Nickolai could not wait to see him.

When the train finally pulled into the station,

Nickolai ran to his son. 'Arkady, my boy!' he cried. 'Come give your papa a hug.'

Arkady was a tall young man in his early twenties. With his fair skin and brown hair, everyone said he looked just like his mother,

who had died years ago. He put one arm around his father and gave him a light hug, nervously looking over his shoulder.

'Father, I would like to introduce you to someone,' Arkady said, stepping aside to let another young man come forward. 'This is my good friend Yevgeny Bazarov. We studied together at university. I have asked him to stay with us, if that is all right with you?'

Nickolai took a step back and looked at Bazarov. Bazarov had long, dark hair that fell past his shoulders and dark eyes. He wore a long, black coat. He looked more like an undertaker than a university graduate. Nickolai was disappointed. He'd been looking forward to spending some time alone with his son after so many years apart. But he smiled at Bazarov and held out his hand to greet him. 'Of course. Any friend of my Arkady is always welcome!' Bazarov looked down at Nickolai's hand and for a moment,

Nickolai thought the young man might not take it. Eventually, Bazarov gave Nickolai's hand a small shake. 'Thank you,' he said quietly.

Nickolai helped load Arkady and Bazarov's cases onto the back of his horse and cart. On their way to Nickolai's estate, Bazarov sat in the back, looking around at the small town with its stores and bustling people. Soon the town melted into open countryside.

Arkady was sitting next to his father on the front of the cart as they drove the horses. 'I am sorry

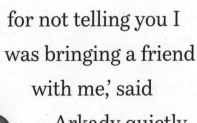

for not telling you I was bringing a friend with me,' said Arkady quietly. It was almost as if he did not want Bazarov to hear what he was saying. 'But you will like Bazarov. He studied science and is going to be a doctor.'

'He doesn't say much,' replied Nickolai.

Arkady smiled. 'Bazarov says only what is necessary. He is a nihilist. As am I, or at least, I am learning to be.'

'A what?' asked Nickolai. He had never heard the word before.

'A nihilist. Nihilists believe that importance should not be placed on anything apart from facts. Emotions do not matter. Manners do not matter. Paintings and sculptures do not matter, and novels and plays do not matter. Only scientific reasoning and research matter.'

Nickolai scratched his head and nodded, although he did not fully understand what his son was talking about.

CHAPTER TWO

When they arrived at Maryino, Nickolai's large estate and Arkady's home, Arkady could not help but feel excited to be back. The house and farmland reminded him of his mother. He'd had many happy times there.

Bazarov's face remained unemotional. It was not the nihilist's way to be impressed or excited by anything. Arkady breathed in the country air coming from the fields that surrounded the stone house. He followed his father as they climbed the stairs that led to the front door.

Once inside, Arkady felt comforted by the grand, old paintings that hung on the walls and the rows of books on every surface. His parents were both great readers and Nickolai had kept all of Arkady's mother's books exactly where she left them.

'Perhaps, when you have settled in, we could have some tea?' said Nickolai, handing his coat and gloves to the butler. 'We have a lot to catch up on, and there is something important I need to discuss with you, Arkady.'

Nickolai turned to go into his study, but he couldn't help noticing the look on Bazarov's face. He was staring at one of the paintings with a look of amusement on his face. It was almost as though he was trying not to laugh.

'You call your father "Papa"?' Bazarov asked. He was sitting on the edge of Arkady's bed, looking around at his friend's childhood bedroom.

'I used to,' said Arkady, blushing. 'Now I call him Father, of course.'

Bazarov gave a small laugh. 'You should call him Nickolai. That is his name,' he said.

Arkady shook his head. Bazarov was determined to make Arkady's life as straightforward and scientific as it could be. While Arkady admired him, and wanted to learn from his new and exciting way of life, there were certain things that Arkady could still not understand.

When Arkady came into the parlour for tea, Nickolai felt a stab of annoyance. Bazarov was with him. He had hoped he would be able to talk to his son alone. 'There is something quite personal

I need to tell you,' said Nickolai, glancing from his son to Bazarov.

'Oh, do not mind me,' said Bazarov. 'I don't believe in the emotion of embarrassment. It serves no purpose in life. I shall sit by the window and read the newspaper while you talk.'

Nickolai nodded to Bazarov, who wandered to a window seat. As his son sat down next to him, Nickolai whispered, 'He is an … *interesting* young man'.

Arkady smiled. 'He's very clever. Perhaps you can learn from him, as I am?' he said.

'Nihilism really is the most interesting subject.'

Nickolai raised an eyebrow. He wasn't sure what this young man with his odd view of life could teach him. Bazarov was almost twice his age! But there were more important things Nickolai needed to talk about now.

'Arkady, do you remember that when your mother died, I employed a housekeeper?' Nickolai began. Arkady nodded as he sipped his tea. 'Well, the housekeeper's daughter used to come and help her. She and I … we became quite close.'

Arkady sat up a little straighter. It was the first time his father had mentioned another woman since his mother had died. He pushed down his feelings of confusion and alarm. He tried to focus on the facts, as Bazarov would. 'Go on,' he said.

'The truth is, I have fallen in love. Her name is Fenichka,' said Nickolai. 'A few months ago, while you were away at university, we had a baby boy. You have a brother.'

Arkady swallowed his tea. He could not help but feel hurt that his father had not told him about

Fenichka, or about his baby brother. They had written to each other while he was away at university and Nickolai could have easily mentioned it. Once again, Arkady took a deep breath and analysed the facts. His father was happy. He had a brother – something he had never had before. These were good things. And his father may not have mentioned it before now because he was worried about Arkady's feelings.

At last, Arkady said, 'I am happy for you, Father. I would like to meet them both.' He trusted the facts of the situation, as a true nihilist would.

Chapter Three

As the days went by, Arkady
met Fenichka and his new baby
brother, Mitya. He liked both of
them immediately and could see
how happy his father
was. Mitya was a happy,
smiling baby, and
Arkady felt
like an older
brother the
second he held
him in his arms.

As Fenichka and Nickolai were not married, Fenichka lived in her own cottage on the estate. She was a little shy of Arkady at first, but she soon saw that he shared his father's warmth and openness.

One evening, while Nickolai, Arkady and Bazarov were having dinner, Nickolai said: 'I would like to marry Fenichka.'

'What is the point of marriage?' asked Bazarov. 'It is just a piece of paper, after all. It means nothing.'

Nickolai shook his head slightly and sipped his drink. 'It is far more than a piece of paper,' he replied.

'I want everyone to know that we are a proper family.'

Bazarov sighed. 'You are a family,' he said. 'I don't see why you need a ceremony in a church to prove it.'

Arkady could see his father was growing tired of Bazarov. 'I think if it makes you happy, Father, then you should do it,' he said, glancing nervously at Bazarov. He wanted his friend to think well of him. Bazarov had spent hours teaching Arkady the rules and principles of Nihilism. He didn't want Bazarov to think he was losing his way.

A moment's silence followed before Bazarov asked: 'May I ask why you read so many novels?'

Nickolai sighed. Since he had arrived at Maryino, Bazarov had questioned why Nickolai enjoyed the paintings on his wall – all art was meaningless. He had also asked why he ate such fine food – food was merely fuel for the body. Nickolai put down his glass and cleared his throat. 'Because I enjoy reading,' he said.

'Then you should read scientific books, or books about history. Novels are stories that someone has invented. They are meaningless,' said Bazarov calmly.

Nickolai looked over at Arkady, knowing how much his son enjoyed reading. But Arkady sat silently, agreeing with Bazarov. Suddenly, Nickolai felt very sad. It was clear

that Arkady was growing away from him. He no longer understood him like he used to when Arkady was a boy.

'I have received a letter from cousin Kolyazin,' Nickolai said, changing the subject. 'You remember he lives in the city, Arkady? Well, the Governor is holding a grand ball next week and Kolyazin has invited me to attend.'

'That will be nice for you, Father,' said Arkady.

'Unfortunately, I won't be attending,' said Nickolai. 'I do not want to leave Fenichka to look after Mitya alone when he is so young. You should go

– and take your friend along.'

Arkady already knew what Bazarov was thinking from the expression on his face: balls were a waste of time. Getting dressed up to eat, drink and dance with people you barely knew would seem very silly to him. However, Arkady also knew that Bazarov having some time away from the house might do him – and Nickolai – some good.

'Think of this,' Arkady said, later that night after his father had gone to bed. 'If we go to the ball, you can turn it into an experiment. You do not have to dance or talk to anyone if you don't want to. You can just observe. Bring your notebook if you like.'

Bazarov sighed, but smiled at his friend. 'If you would like to go so much, then we shall,' he said. 'I can see you have a long way to go before becoming a true nihilist, my friend.'

Arkady smiled. 'But I am learning,' he said. 'Even nihilists need to eat and drink, you know!'

CHAPTER FOUR

Cousin Kolyazin was a cheerful man. He was about the same age as Nickolai and wore bright, expensive clothes. He was delighted to see his young relative, and the strange young man with the long dark hair whom he had brought with him.

'The Governor's Ball is one of the highlights of the year!' said Kolyazin as they climbed into his carriage. 'Everyone will be there. Some of them you will know, Arkady. Everyone is excited to see Anna Odintsov.'

'Who is that?' asked Arkady.

'A young widow with a large fortune,' said Kolyazin. 'Her husband bought an estate nearby before he died and now she lives there with her sister. I've met her once already. She is very beautiful.'

'What does beauty mean?' said Bazarov. 'The fact that her eyes and nose and ears are arranged in a certain way does not have any impact on who she is as a person.'

Kolyazin was too excited to notice Bazarov's grumpy tone. 'We'll see!' he said, clapping his hands. 'Perhaps even *you* will fall under her spell!'

The ballroom was lit up with hundreds of candles, the light bouncing off gigantic mirrors that hung over the fireplaces. The floor was filled with swirling dresses and every seat was taken by well-dressed guests.

Arkady felt excited to be there. He hadn't been to a ball like this since before he went to university. However, he knew that he shouldn't be impressed by such a trivial thing as a ball. He tried to keep his face straight in case Bazarov was watching him. But Bazarov, it seemed, was captivated by something else. *Someone* else.

'Ah, I see you have spotted Anna Odintsov already,' said Kolyazin, nudging Bazarov in the ribs. Anna Odintsov was wearing a shimmering silver dress.

Her blonde hair was elegantly piled on top of her head, and she was talking to a large group of people who were all battling for her attention.

Bazarov coughed, his face turning red. 'I was simply thinking about how bright it is in here,' he said hurriedly. 'The cost for the candles alone must be very high.'

In a flash, Kolyazin disappeared. He returned moments later with Anna on his arm. 'Let me introduce you to my young nephew, Arkady Kirsanov, and his friend Yevgeny Bazarov,' Kolyazin said with a smile. 'They have recently graduated from St Petersburg University.'

Anna looked impressed. 'A pair of scholars,' she said. 'I am very pleased to meet you.'

Suddenly the orchestra, who were placed at the far end of the ballroom, started playing. 'Would you like to dance?' asked Bazarov, reaching out his hand towards Anna.

Arkady's eyes widened. He had never known Bazarov to dance the entire time he had known him. The only time Bazarov mentioned dancing was to say how pointless it was. Anna accepted his hand and Bazarov led her to the dance floor. Arkady marvelled at how graceful his friend was. He had tied his long hair back for the occasion and looked almost gentlemanly.

'What have you been studying, sir?' asked Anna politely, as she danced with Bazarov.

'Science,' he replied. 'I wish to study medicine next, and perhaps become a doctor.'

Anna watched Bazarov's face. He was a good dancer, but he did not seem to be enjoying himself much. 'Do you dance often?' she asked.

'No,' Bazarov replied bluntly. 'Forgive me, but I find the act pointless.'

Anna laughed. 'Then why did you ask me to dance?'

Bazarov could not reply. He had asked her to dance because he found her captivating. He had to admit that Kolyazin was right: Anna Odintsov was beautiful.

CHAPTER FIVE

The ball carried on late into the night. Arkady, Bazarov and Kolyazin found themselves huddled in a corner with Anna, and the four talked and danced for hours. Arkady watched as Bazarov's smile grew bigger and bigger the more time that passed.

'I am exhausted!' said Anna happily as the ball came to an end. 'It is not fair that there is one of me and three of you.

I have danced three times as many dances!'

After they said their goodbyes, the three men climbed back into their carriage with aching feet. 'See, did I not tell you that Anna was the most heavenly young woman?' said Kolyazin.

'She is very beautiful,' agreed Arkady.

'She is too old for you, my friend,' said Bazarov.

Arkady frowned. 'She is only a couple of years older than me,' he said. 'And she is older than you, too.' Bazarov waved his hand dismissively. 'Anyway, she invited us all to her hotel tomorrow for tea before she leaves the city.'

Bazarov sat up straight. 'She did?' he said. Arkady nodded and smiled at his friend. It was odd to see Bazarov's cool and calm composure broken for once.

'She'll be keen to get back to her sister at Nikolskoye,' said Kolyazin. 'Since her husband died, it has been just the two of them in that

great house with a grand fortune
to spend.'

Bazarov did not care how much
money Anna had. Money meant
nothing to him. All he knew was
that he wanted to spend more time
with her.

The following day, Bazarov and
Arkady went to the hotel where
Anna was staying. Kolyazin had
business to do in the city, so he left
them to make their visit alone.

In the café of the Grand Hotel in
the centre of the city, Anna Odintsov

was surrounded by luggage. She smiled happily when she saw the two young men she had met at the Governor's Ball the previous evening. 'You have just caught me!' she said. 'My carriage will be here in half an hour to take me back to Nikolskoye.'

'Please forgive my cousin,' Arkady said. 'He could not join us this morning. But now you have us all to yourself!'

Bazarov frowned at Arkady. He was acting foolishly, and Bazarov suspected that Arkady might have the same feelings for Anna that he did.

'But it is not enough time to get to know you properly,' said Anna. 'Why don't you both come to stay with me at Nikolskoye? It is far too big just for me and my sister. We could do with some company.'

Arkady looked at Bazarov cautiously. He was certain his friend would say no to the invitation. Bazarov did not pay calls on ladies, much less stay at their houses. It distracted him from his work.

To Arkady's great surprise, Bazarov replied: 'We would be delighted.'

Later that day, the friends said goodbye to Kolyazin, who was quite jealous of their invitation. He would have liked to have seen inside Anna's house for himself. Then they packed up their things and made the short journey into the countryside to Nikolskoye.

Chapter Six

Nikolskoye was a beautiful house with perfect gardens. It was much larger than Arkady's family home. In fact, it made his own estate looks quite run down in comparison.

There were stone carvings around each window and a fountain outside the front of the house that was bigger than any Arkady or Bazarov had ever seen.

The friends were welcomed by a stern-looking butler in uniform. He took Bazarov's long coat as though it were something he had just picked off the floor. 'Madame is this way,' he said in a cold voice, as he led them along a long marble corridor.

Anna was sitting in a large room flooded with light. The fireplace was lit and a pretty tea set with several cakes was laid out on a table. 'I thought I heard a carriage,' said Anna happily. 'You are right on time!'

Bazarov felt a surge of happiness the moment he saw Anna, but he tried hard not to show it. Arkady, too, was happy to see Anna again, although he noticed her eyes were focused on Bazarov when she spoke.

At that moment, another young woman entered the room, followed by a large white dog. 'Let me introduce you to Katya, my younger sister,' said Anna, getting up and putting an arm around

Katya's waist. 'And this is Fifi.'
Anna ruffled the white fur on the
dog's head as he sniffed the two
men curiously.

Katya was very like her sister, though her hair was darker and she was at least five years younger. As the butler served tea and offered cake, Katya petted her dog and occasionally smiled and nodded at her sister's new friends. She preferred to listen to the conversation rather than take part in it.

'After lunch I would like to show you my garden,' said Anna. Again, she was talking directly to Bazarov. 'We have a herb garden. Many of the plants we grow are used in medicines, I believe.'

Bazarov smiled and nodded. He was thrilled to be asked to spend some time alone with Anna. 'That would be very educational, thank you,' he replied.

'Perhaps Katya could show you some of your mother's letters, Arkady?'

Arkady put down his teacup with a start. 'I'm sorry?' he asked, confused. 'You have letters from my mother?'

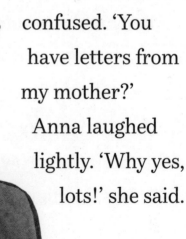

Anna laughed lightly. 'Why yes, lots!' she said.

'I realised last night why your name was so familiar to me. Our mother and your mother were childhood friends. They did not see each other much after they got married, but they stayed in touch. When our mother died, Katya and I kept a chest of her letters. I am so happy to know you, Arkady. It feels like a little connection to our mother.'

Arkady felt thrilled, but also slightly disappointed. He would love to read his mother's letters, but he'd been hoping Anna might want to spend some time with him herself, rather than Katya.

'What a wonderful discovery,' Arkady said at last. 'If you have the time, Katya, that would be very nice.'

And so, after a delicious lunch, Arkady and Katya parted ways with Bazarov and Anna to spend their afternoon.

CHAPTER SEVEN

As the weeks went by, Anna and
Bazarov found more excuses to
spend time alone with one another.
She showed him the gardens each
day, and they looked through the
telescope her late husband had
given her to gaze at the stars.

This left Arkady to be entertained
by Katya. To his surprise, he found
that he liked her more each day.
She was quieter than her sister,
but she was clever and kind.

The first afternoon they spent together was in the attic of the great house, surrounded by Arkady's mother's letters. Seeing her handwriting was a great comfort to Arkady. He laughed as he read stories of himself as a baby, and smiled as he learnt about his mother's day-to-day life at Maryino.

After showing Arkady his mother's letters, Katya took him to the library. Without Bazarov around, Arkady confessed that he

used to love reading novels. Katya
showed him her favourite books
and poems, and they discovered
they had a lot in common. Arkady
even grew fond of Fifi, who followed
them everywhere in hope of
a head scratch.

While Arkady grew happier and happier at Nikolskoye, Bazarov became filled with confusion. The more time he spent with Anna, the stronger his feelings grew towards her. He had never felt the rush of emotions he felt when she was nearby. Despite his determination that such feelings were silly, he knew that he was falling in love.

But Bazarov wanted to be a faithful nihilist. Nihilists did not follow young ladies around in a cloud of romance. He felt silly and frustrated with himself. He knew that if he stayed much longer, his belief in nihilism would be tested.

As much as he wanted to stay with Anna, Bazarov knew he had to leave Nikolskoye.

Bazarov waited until Arkady and Katya had gone to bed one evening. Then he told Anna that he would be leaving the next day.

Anna felt a stab of disappointment. She had enjoyed spending her days with Bazarov. He was the most interesting young man she had ever met. When they walked in the garden or he explained something scientific to her, she felt happier

than she had for many years.
'Why must you leave now?' Anna
asked, trying to keep her voice
light.

'I must go and see my parents,'
Bazarov replied. 'I have not seen
them since I graduated from
university.'

This much was true. Bazarov
had not seen his parents for many
years. But the real reason he
wanted to leave was to remove
himself from Anna before his
feelings grew any stronger.

'I will miss you,' said Anna,
gazing into the fire.

Bazarov stared at her. The light from the flames lit up her face and made her look even more beautiful. 'I will miss you too,' Bazarov said, despite himself. He wrestled with his feelings. He wanted nothing more than to stay with Anna forever, but that would mean giving up his beliefs. Perhaps it would be worth it? Suddenly, Bazarov moved to sit next to Anna and held her hand.

'I love you,' he said.

To his surprise, Anna pulled her hand away. 'I'm sorry, Bazarov. I can't be with you!' she said, quickly standing up and rushing from the room.

Bazarov's heart felt like it had split in two. He had thought that Anna felt the same way for him as he did for her. He must have been wrong. He had betrayed his nihilistic beliefs and given in to emotion for nothing.

Bazarov flew up the stairs of the  grand house and into Arkady's bedroom. Arkady was reading in bed and jumped up when his friend entered.

Bazarov looked upset – something Arkady had never seen before. 'Whatever is the matter?' asked Arkady.

'I must leave tomorrow morning,' Bazarov said, sitting heavily at the end of Arkady's bed. 'I have fallen in love with Anna.'

Arkady had suspected that his friend had fallen in love, but he never expected him to admit it.

'It is all right to feel love, Bazarov,' said Arkady. 'Even men of science get married.'

Bazarov shook his head. 'She does not feel the same way as me,' he replied. 'I must go away and forget this place. There is no point in dwelling on something that has no future.'

Arkady was surprised that Anna did not feel the same way. He had noticed the way she looked at Bazarov. 'Are you certain?' Arkady asked.

'I am,' replied Bazarov firmly. 'I will go to my parents' house tomorrow. You are more than welcome to join me, but I understand if you would rather stay here. My parents' home is far smaller than this.'

Arkady smiled sadly. 'You are my friend, Bazarov. I would like to meet your parents.'

The following morning, Bazarov and Arkady said their goodbyes. Bazarov spoke few words, but thanked Anna for having them. Arkady was sad to be leaving Katya and he promised to write to her. Arkady noticed tears welling in Anna's eyes as she waved them off.

Chapter Eight

Doctor and Mrs Bazarov lived in a smart townhouse in a small town just an hour away from St Petersburg. The town was run-down and there were people huddled around fires in the streets. Bazarov looked straight ahead as their carriage rolled through the town, while Arkady looked out of the window at the boarded-up shops and houses.

Eventually the carriage turned onto a more pleasant street and

stopped in front of a house with a
man and woman standing outside.
The man was tall and dressed in a
brown woollen suit. His hair was
neat and he had a warm, friendly
face. The woman's face was lined but
happy. She wore a shawl around her
shoulders and her grey hair fell in
a long plait over her shoulder. She
looked half the size of her husband.

As soon as Bazarov had stepped from the carriage, his parents covered him in hugs and kisses. 'My son! My son!' cried the man. 'You are home at last!'

Arkady smiled at the scene as he took their luggage from the carriage driver. When Bazarov was finally released, he introduced his friend. 'Mother, Father, this is Arkady Kirsanov.'

Doctor Bazarov kissed Arkady on both cheeks. 'You are very welcome here!' he said.

Mrs Bazarov waved a small hand and beckoned Arkady inside.

'Come, come!' she said. 'We have lunch ready for you. You are both far too skinny!'

Over lunch, Arkady marvelled at Doctor and Mrs Bazarov. He could not understand how his friend, who was always so calm and measured, could have been brought up by these people. They were loud and friendly. They asked questions and told stories.

'You would not think of it to look at him,' said Doctor Bazarov, filling up Arkady's glass. 'But Yevgeny was a tiny little thing when he was younger.'

Bazarov shook his head and blushed. Arkady laughed at his friend's embarrassment. 'But he was always so serious!' said Mrs Bazarov. 'So clever and so determined. We knew he would do well.'

'Mother, that is enough,' Bazarov said. Arkady noticed that he called his parents 'Mother' and 'Father', and not by their real names as he had once advised Arkady to do with his. 'Arkady has not come here to hear my life story.'

'Why not?' exclaimed Mrs Bazarov. 'We are so proud of you.

We tell your story to anyone who will sit still long enough to hear it.'

Bazarov and Arkady spent the afternoon helping Doctor Bazarov in his surgery. Bazarov studied the cases that his father could not diagnose, and Arkady helped with the filing.

'You boys are so helpful, I won't be able to do without you when you go!' said the doctor.

'We can only stay a few days,' said Bazarov.

Arkady noticed Doctor Bazarov's face fall slightly, before he smiled again. 'Oh, well. It is nice to see you for however long we can.'

That evening, Arkady and Bazarov retired to the room they were sharing on the top floor of the house. 'We can stay longer than a few days,' said Arkady. 'You have not seen your parents for a long time. They might want you to stay.'

Bazarov sighed and rubbed his head. 'My parents are too much for me,' he said. 'All my life I have been unable to understand them. They seem so happy and content to live a small life, but I always knew I wanted something different. When I went to university, I found nihilism and it suited me. I had lived my life surrounded by too much emotion – nihilism offered me a life with no emotion.'

Arkady nodded. He felt he now understood his friend so much more than he had before. 'Your parents love you,' said Arkady, kindly. 'And that has made them happy.'

'But what good has that done them?' said Bazarov, becoming angry. 'My father could be one of the best doctors in Russia, but he is too emotional. He gets involved in people's lives instead of looking at the facts!'

Arkady could see that his friend was upset. 'Let us stay one more day, then we can return to Maryino. You left some of your work there. You can continue it in peace and I can see my father. Perhaps that will clear your mind?'

Bazarov agreed. Maryino was quiet and, best of all, it was far enough away from Anna and his parents that he could concentrate on what was important.

Mrs Bazarov could not stop crying when Arkady and Bazarov left for Maryino. Doctor Bazarov also had tears in his eyes. 'You are the best thing in our lives,' said the doctor as he hugged his son tightly. 'Come back soon.'

Bazarov pulled away from his parents and climbed into the

carriage. Arkady thanked Doctor
and Mrs Bazarov for having him
stay at their house. 'Look after my
boy,' said Mrs Bazarov.

'I will,' replied Arkady.

CHAPTER NINE

The journey back to Maryino was quiet. Bazarov did not want to talk. His mind was full of questions.

Bazarov wanted to be a true nihilist. For him, this meant that feelings and emotions were not important. He did not expect to fall in love with Anna and he had gone to his parents to forget her. Instead, he was faced with his parents' overbearing love for him.

Arkady could see that his friend was upset, so he left him to think. Soon, Arkady felt his own mind being tugged back to Katya. He had thought of her every day since he and Bazarov had left Nikolskoye. Now that they were apart, it was like a piece of him was missing.

Arkady stared out of the carriage window, feeling comforted when

the land around Maryino came into view. He was also surprised when he noticed how run-down some of the farm buildings had become. His father had always managed the estate and the farmland so well, and Arkady wondered what had gone wrong in the years that he had been away.

Nickolai was overjoyed to see his son again. He gave Arkady a big hug, and Arkady hugged him back. Bazarov watched and marvelled at how easily Arkady showed love to his father.

Bazarov excused himself almost immediately and went to find the papers he had been working on before they left. Arkady was pleased. He wanted to talk to his father alone.

'Papa, may I ask you something?' asked Arkady. They were sitting in his father's study.

Piles of paper covered the large mahogany desk.

'Of course, my boy,' Nickolai replied.

Arkady took a deep breath. 'Is everything all right with the estate? On the way here I noticed some of the farm buildings look like they need repairing, and some of the fields are empty. Shouldn't they be full of corn by now?'

The smile on Nickolai's face faded. He had wanted to keep the truth from

his son for as long as possible. Nickolai had been struggling to keep on top of his work. The older he became, the harder he found managing the estate all by himself. It was hard for him to admit this, because he wanted Arkady to see him as his strong, capable Papa.

'It is time you knew the truth,' said Nickolai with a sigh. 'I cannot keep up anymore. The farmers are complaining and work is not being done. If I don't get help soon, I am afraid I might have to sell the estate. I want to marry Fenichka and provide a good home for her and little Mitya, but I am not as young as I was.'

Arkady put his hand on his father's shoulder. Studying nihilism with Bazarov had taught him to look at facts rather than emotions. Here Arkady realised that he could and should look at both.

'Papa,' Arkady said, 'I think I have an idea.'

Chapter Ten

Arkady decided that he would live at Maryino and help his father with the estate. When he was at university, this had felt like the last thing he would ever want to do. He had grand plans to commit to nihilism and travel the country with Bazarov. But so much had changed over the last few weeks. For one, Arkady had felt so happy to be back at his old home. For another, he now knew that he wanted to get married.

He also knew *who* he wanted to get married to.

When Arkady told his father that he would stay and help on the estate, Nickolai was thrilled. 'My darling boy, do you know what this means?' he said, taking Arkady's hand. 'I do not have to sell, and I can marry Fenichka. Best of all, you will be here. We can work alongside each other! I cannot tell you how happy this makes me.'

Arkady felt happier and more certain of his future than he had for some time. He had trusted his head, but also his heart.

'Father, there is one last thing
I need to do before I can start
working on the estate properly,'
Arkady said. 'Do you remember a
friend of Mama's called Madame
Lotkev? She had two daughters
called Anna and Katya.'

Nickolai frowned in concentration.
'The name is familiar,' he said, trying
to remember. 'It sounds like an old
schoolfriend she used to have.'

'That's right. I wonder, do you
have any of Mama's old letters?'
asked Arkady.

'There is a chest in the attic,
I believe. This is all very curious!'

said Nickolai, chuckling at his son's odd request.

Arkady smiled. 'Thank you, Papa,' he said, as he ran up to the attic to search for the letters from Katya's mother.

Bazarov continued to study in his room. He had taken some of his father's medical books with him when he left home, and he spent hours going through them. He only came downstairs at mealtimes and was quiet and polite. He no longer questioned Nickolai's enjoyment of paintings and books.

After dinner one evening, Arkady asked Bazarov to stay with him by the fire, instead of returning to his room to study.

'I have made a decision,' Arkady said. 'In fact, I have made two decisions.'

Bazarov nodded. 'That is good,' he replied. 'I hope you have given these decisions plenty of thought?'

'I have. The first is that I am going to go back to Nikolskoye to see Katya,' said Arkady.

At the sound of Anna's home, Bazarov looked at the fire, worried his feelings for Anna might show on his face. 'I hope you will allow me not to accompany you,' said Bazarov.

'Of course,' replied Arkady. He knew that seeing Anna again would make Bazarov unhappy. 'My father is more than happy for you to stay here. My second decision is a rather big one. I have decided to stay here and help my father on the estate. He cannot manage on his own and I like it here.' Arkady smiled to himself and added: 'I suppose you will think I am not a true nihilist now. I have let my feelings guide my decisions.'

Bazarov sighed and sat back in his chair. 'You are a clever man, my friend,' Bazarov said. 'And a good man. All this time I thought I was teaching you the best way to live. Perhaps I should have been learning from *you*.'

Arkady and Bazarov talked until it was late. Although Arkady knew

they would always be friends,
he and Bazarov were headed in
different directions. Arkady's life
now centred around Maryino,
helping his father, and one more
thing: Katya. Although he was not
brave enough to confess
it to Bazarov just yet,
Arkady knew that he
wanted to spend his
life with Katya.

CHAPTER ELEVEN

The journey to Nikolskoye seemed
to take a lifetime. Arkady could not
wait to see Katya again.
When he finally arrived,
Katya ran out of the
house to greet him,
her enormous dog
Fifi running closely
behind her.

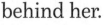

Katya laughed at the size of the
large trunk Arkady was carrying. 'Is
that full of clothes?' she asked. 'How
long are you intending to stay?'

'I have brought a surprise for you
and Anna,' said Arkady, smiling.

Katya and Arkady waited in
the parlour for Anna to join them.
When she did, Arkady opened the
trunk he had brought. 'When I was
last here, you were kind enough
to show me the letters my mother
sent to yours,' Arkady said, placing
a pile of yellowing envelopes
between the sisters. 'It was such a
comfort to me to see my mother's

 writing and hear her voice in my head. I thought it would be nice for you to do the same. These are the letters from your mother to mine.'

Katya and Anna looked at the letters, then at each other. Their eyes filled with tears. 'Thank you,' said Katya, taking Arkady's hand. 'Thank you so much!'

Katya and Anna spent the day reading their mother's letters. Although the memories were tinged with sadness,

they laughed as they remembered
the birthdays and holidays their
mother wrote about in her letters.
They felt lucky to have them and felt
close to their mother once more.

At dinner, Anna asked Arkady nervously why Bazarov had not come with him.

'Bazarov is committed to his studies right now,' said Arkady, politely. 'But he said to pass on his regards.' Arkady did not want to say the truth: that Bazarov could not bear to see Anna again after she had rejected him.

After dinner, Anna went to bed early and left Arkady and Katya to talk. Arkady's heart started to pound in his chest. He was going to ask Katya to marry him. He felt his palms become hot and sweaty, his neck become cold and his knees tremble. Even Bazarov would have to admit that his emotions at that moment were real. They had such an effect on his body!

'Katya,' Arkady began softly. 'There is another reason why I wanted to come and see you.'

Katya smiled and stroked Fifi's sleeping head as it rested in her lap. 'What is that?' she asked.

'I would like to ask you to marry me,' Arkady said. 'I fell in love with you on our last visit. I want to spend the rest of my life with you.'

Katya's eyes widened with joy. She had counted each day she had been apart from Arkady. She had treasured each letter he had sent her. He was the only man she had ever felt anything more than friendship for. 'Oh, Arkady!' she said. 'Of course I will marry you!'

Arkady thought his heart would burst. He was truly happy.

Chapter Twelve

Later that evening, Arkady wrote
to his father and Bazarov to tell
them the happy news. A few days
later, he had replies from both of
them. Nickolai's letter was full
of congratulations and happy
thoughts. He could not wait to
meet his future daughter-in-
law. But Arkady trembled as he
opened Bazarov's letter. He did
not know how his friend would
react to the news.

My dear friend,

Once I would have thought that marriage was the most pointless activity on earth. Now, however, I can see how it is good for some people. Perhaps if I had won Anna's love I would have married, too. I am happy for you.

I also have news. I have decided to leave Maryino to go back to my parents' house. I have been thinking of them a great deal since you told me how you wanted to help your father. Perhaps the greatest way to learn is to learn from our parents.

By the time this letter reaches you, I will be on my way. I wish you nothing but the best.

Yours in friendship,
Bazarov

Arkady held the letter to his chest. At university, Arkady had believed that Bazarov knew everything. Nihilism had seemed the best way to live his life. And yet, so much had happened to them over the past few weeks to change their minds.

Arkady had realised that home and family were more important than anything else in the world. He would be forever thankful to Bazarov for teaching him the ways of nihilism. And he would look at the facts, as well as his feelings, in every situation that presented itself to him.

Bazarov had also learnt to question his trust in nihilism. He still wanted to believe in truth and facts, but he had started to realise that there was more to life than just this. His love for Anna and admiration for his parents had shown him that.

Doctor and Mrs Bazarov were overjoyed to have their son home once again. They were happier still when he declared that he would like to stay with them and study to become a doctor like his father.

Bazarov helped his father each day as he saw patients in his surgery and visited their homes. He started to see how all sorts of different people lived their lives.

In the evenings, Bazarov would take a medical book and sit by his mother at the fireplace. She would

sew or read, and occasionally look up at her son as he read by the glow of the fire.

One day, Doctor Bazarov came into the surgery with a sad look on his face. 'A family is very ill. They have a serious illness called typhus.'

Bazarov looked at his father and saw how tired he was from a busy day. 'I will go and see them,' said Bazarov, taking his father's medical bag. 'I know the treatments. I can help them.'

Doctor Bazarov agreed. 'Thank you, son,' he said, sitting heavily at his desk. 'I will ask Mama to start the dinner for when you return.'

CHAPTER THIRTEEN

When Bazarov went to see the
family with typhus, he was
shocked. He knew they were very
ill, but he was not prepared to see
each family member covered in a
rash and shaking from fever.

Bazarov went from bed to bed in
the tiny house, giving each person
medicine. Those who could speak
thanked him. Those who were too
ill to talk tried to smile. Bazarov
was touched. Even when they were

suffering, this family remembered their manners. It was important to them to be grateful and polite. This poor family were teaching Bazarov more about how to live than he had ever learnt at university. This was *real* life, Bazarov realised.

When he left, Bazarov felt as though he had done some good. He had to admit that it made him happy to be able to make a difference, no matter how small. As soon as he returned home, he wrote to Arkady about his experience.

A few days later, Bazarov started to feel unwell. Doctor Bazarov knew the signs – Bazarov had caught typhus.

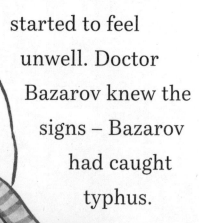

The fever made him feel terrible. Soon he was too weak to move out of bed. Bazarov took the same medicine he had given the family, but still his condition got worse.

'Father,' Bazarov asked after two days in bed. 'Please send for Anna Odintsov.' Bazarov feared that he would not recover. He needed to see Anna one last time.

Although he had never written to someone as rich and powerful as Anna, Doctor Bazarov did as his son asked. He told Anna that his son was dying and to come quickly. When Anna arrived at the little house a few days later, her eyes were red as though she had been crying. Doctor and Mrs Bazarov welcomed her and showed her to Bazarov's room. They marvelled at how their son knew such a fine lady.

Anna sat by Bazarov's bedside and held his hand. She was shocked to see how he had changed. His face was pale and he had lost the sparkle from his eyes. 'I am so sorry, Bazarov,' whispered Anna. 'I was foolish to turn you away when you told me you loved me.'

Bazarov looked at Anna, too exhausted to speak.

'I am like you,' Anna said with a sad smile. 'I look at the facts of the situation. The fact is that I was not always rich. I thought I needed to marry someone with money, to support my sister and the house. But now Katya is getting married,

as I am sure you know. I don't need to worry about her anymore.'

Bazarov nodded slightly. He wanted to tell Anna that he understood. That none of that mattered now. It only mattered that she was there with him.

'I wish I had not made you leave, Bazarov,' Anna continued. 'The days we spent together were the happiest of my life. I loved you and I turned you away. Can you ever forgive me?'

Bazarov squeezed Anna's hand as tightly as he could. He nodded once more, then closed his eyes.

Doctor and Mrs Bazarov joined Anna in their son's room. They stayed with him until the last breath left his body, surrounding him with love.

EPILOGUE

Arkady and Katya, Nickolai and
Fenichka were married in a double
wedding ceremony. It was a joyous

day, even though Arkady wished Bazarov could have been there.

The two couples worked hard to get the Maryino estate back to how it used to be. They mended the farm buildings and sewed the fields with crops. Soon, Arkady and Katya had a son whom they called Nickolai after Arkady's father. Katya and Fenichka became the closest of friends, and Anna visited them often.

After Bazarov's death, Arkady promised that he would try each day to remember what his friend had taught him. He still analysed each situation by looking at the facts, but he no longer dismissed what his heart was telling him.

Anna married a lawyer from a good family with plenty of money. Even though she did not feel as much love for him as she had for Bazarov, her new husband was a kind man. She was happy.

Doctor and Mrs Bazarov visited Bazarov's grave in their small town's cemetery each day.

Although they were devastated to have lost him, they were proud of the man their son had been.

Eugene Onegin is young, handsome, rich … and bored. Nothing impresses him: not his grand house filled with expensive furniture, not the glittering balls he attends, not the sumptuous dinners he eats. When his uncle dies, leaving him his rundown estate, Eugene moves to the countryside. Here he meets the lively and intelligent Lensky, and the beautiful, quiet Tatyana.

Will Eugene grasp this opportunity for a new and happy life, or will his bad attitude get in the way?

Rocket

SILLY SAUSAGE

Sausage in Trouble

Michaela Morgan
& Dee Shulman

A & C Black • London

For Lulu, the real little Sausage

Rockets series:

CROOK CATCHERS - Karen Wallace & Judy Brown

MOTLEY'S CREW - Margaret Ryan & Margaret Chamberlain

MR CROC - Frank Rodgers

MRS MAGIC - Wendy Smith

MY FUNNY FAMILY - Colin West

ROVER - Chris Powling & Scoular Anderson

SILLY SAUSAGE - Michaela Morgan & Dee Shulman

WIZARD'S BOY - Scoular Anderson

First paperback edition 2001
First published 2001 in hardback by
A & C Black (Publishers) Ltd
35 Bedford Row, London WC1R 4JH

Text copyright © 2001 Michaela Morgan
Illustrations copyright © 2001 Dee Shulman

The right of Michaela Morgan and Dee Shulman
to be identified as author and illustrator of this
work has been asserted by them in accordance
with the Copyright, Designs and Patents Act 1988.

ISBN 0-7136-5476-7

A CIP catalogue record for this book is available
from the British Library.

Printed and bound by G. Z. Printek, Bilbao, Spain.

Chapter One

There are all sorts of dogs in the world.

Some dogs are soft and furry.

Some dogs are big and burly.

Some dogs are very, very small.

But there is one dog that is very, very long and very, very low and as plump as a sausage.

His name is Sausage.

7

Sausage is a friendly dog.
He likes playing around.

He likes lying around...

...and he likes eating –
especially sausages.

He's not a fierce dog.
He's not a fast dog.
He's a friendly dog – but he does have
a few little problems...

...like getting
stuck in doors.

OUCH!

Chapter Two

Some people call Sausage...

... Silly Sausage!

The cats think he's very silly indeed.

There are two cats in Sausage's house.
One is called Fitz.
The other is called Spatz.

Fitz is a very sleek and smart cat. A black and white cat with fine twitchy whiskers.

Spatz is a burly ginger tom.

He loves to fight.

12

Both of the cats are snooty. They can stare without blinking...

...and they stare at Sausage.

'What can
you do?'
they asked
Sausage.

'Can you look cuddly like this?'

14

'Can you look
cute like this?'

'Can you look
elegant like this?'

15

Sausage tried his best...

...but he wasn't good at any of those things.

'Not much ornamental value then,' sneered the snooty cats...

'How many mice have you caught?' they asked.

How many voles?

FITZ'S VOLE SCORE
卌 卌
卌 II

How many moles?

SPATZ'S MOLE SCORE
卌 卌
卌 III

I did catch a cold once.

18

'None,' said Sausage, sadly.
'None at all.'

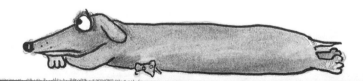

'Not much of a hunter then,'
sneered the cats.

19

'How high can you climb?'

Can you climb that hedge?

Can you climb this wall?

'I've only ever climbed the stairs,' Sausage admitted.

'Not much of a climber then,' sneered the cats.

21

'He's no good at all,' the cats decided. 'He really is a silly sausage!'

And they both put their noses in the air and stalked off.

Sausage was very sad.

Chapter Three

Gran didn't think Sausage was silly at all. 'One day he'll show you all!' she said.

'He's very good at finding sausages,'
said Elly, 'and he's very good at eating
them all up quickly.'

'All he does is eat and lie around,'
said Jack.

'He doesn't run very well.'

'He doesn't fetch very well.
He doesn't catch very well.'

'He's just a lazy, lying-around sort
of dog.'

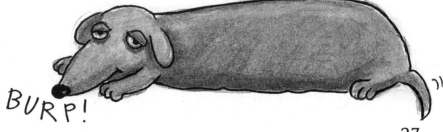

27

'So he is,' said Gran, 'but he keeps my neck warm...'

'...and my toes toasty...'

28

'...and he stops the cold air coming in the doors.'

'Don't worry, Sausage,' said Gran, 'you are not just a silly sausage.'

> You are a heart-warming, foot-warming, kind-hearted sausage, and one day, everyone will think so too.

'I hope so,' thought Sausage.

Chapter Four

One night the family were all tucked up in their beds. Sausage was dozing by the door.

He was dreaming of bones... and biscuits... and sausages. Heaps and heaps of sizzling meaty sausages.

The cats were napping.

Upstairs, dad was snoring.

Mum was fast asleep.

The children were dreaming of adventures.

Gran had unplugged her hearing aid.

Everyone was fast asleep.

So no one heard...

...the footsteps...

...the whispering...

Got the torch?

Got the sack?

...the window opening...

squeak

32

...and the burglars sneaking in.

Chapter Five

It was up to Sausage to be the guard dog...

...the watch dog...

...the police dog.

It was up to
Sausage to
save the day.

STOP! In the name of the law!

Unfortunately, Sausage didn't
hear a thing.
He was fast asleep.

The burglars tiptoed around.

They took the
television...

...they took
the video...

...and quite a lot of other things too.

The burglars started to tiptoe out of the house. They were very pleased with themselves.

But they didn't see Sausage.
Sausage was lying by the door.
He was so low they couldn't see him.
He was so long they couldn't miss him.

They tiptoed and they tiptoed and then they tripped right over the low-lying dog.

CRASH!

Everybody was startled.

...so was Sausage.
'Woof, woof!' he barked.

Chapter Six

In a moment everyone was up.
Mum was phoning the police.

Dad was
standing
guard.

Gran was hitting
the burglars with
an umbrella...

...and the children were tying them up...

...and everyone was saying 'Well done Sausage!'

Sausage felt proud.

Soon he felt even prouder. Everyone in the neighbourhood talked about him.

45

Sausage felt wonderful. He held his head high and trotted around the neighbourhood.

Gran said she had been right all along.

This little dog is a heart-warming, foot-warming, toe-toasting, draught-excluding, low-lying, thief-tripping **hero!**

So she gave him a big bowl of sizzling sausages as a reward.